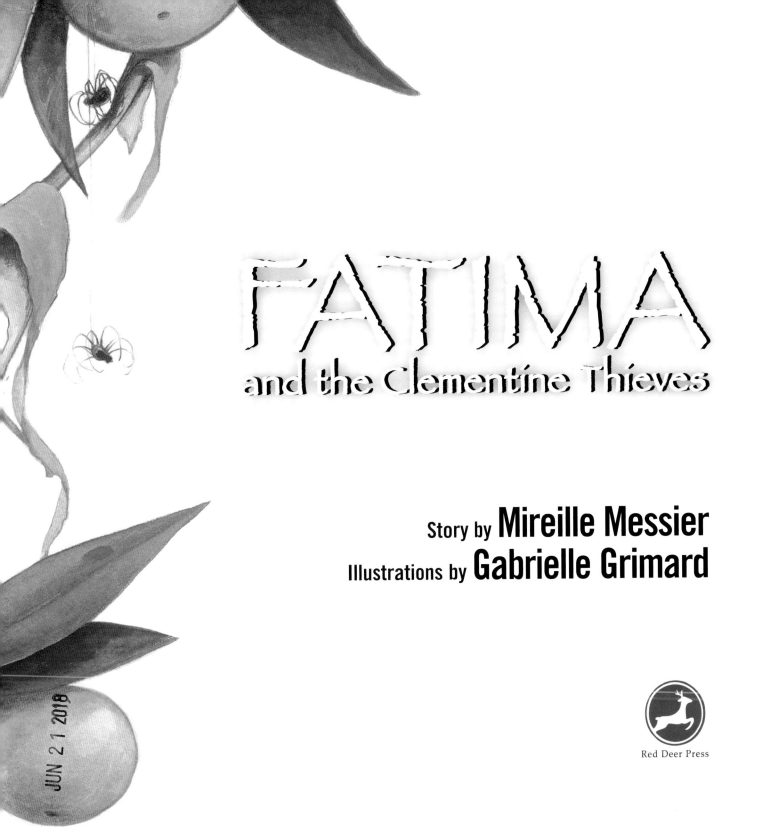

FATIMA
and the Clementine Thieves

Story by **Mireille Messier**

Illustrations by **Gabrielle Grimard**

Red Deer Press

Every day, Fatima helps her grandfather in their clementine orchard.

When it is time to rest, Fatima stops her work and peels clementines in the shape of flowers. She shares them with her friends, the spiders:

"You may be small, but thanks to you there are no bugs eating our trees!"

As the sun reaches the top of the highest cedar, Fatima joins her grandfather. He is particularly happy today.

"Tomorrow we will finally have enough ripe clementines to sell them at the market," says Grandfather. "Then, we can celebrate! We will buy fish and pistachios and olives!"

"And sweet almond paste?" asks Fatima.

"If there's enough money left, yes!" he answers with a smile.

Fatima longs for tomorrow to come. She will climb the ladder to the highest rung and pick the fruit that grows closest to the sun. Those are the sweetest and best clementines.

When she finally falls asleep, Fatima dreams that the moon is a grapefruit.

At sunrise,
Fatima jumps
from her bed and
runs down the stairs.
"Shall I get the
baskets?" she asks.
But Grandfather does
not answer. He stares out the
window, his fists tightly clenched.
Fatima follows his angry gaze. And what
she sees turns her heart to marmalade …

During the night, trees were broken and fruit was stolen.

"Our harvest is ruined," she says to the spiders. "Without the money from the clementines, we won't have enough to buy food or clothes."

The spiders weave a special web to cheer up their friend. But Fatima is too sad to notice.

The next morning, the orchard is filled with newly broken trees and more trampled fruit.

"Tonight, we will guard the land," fumes Grandfather. "I must know who these clementine thieves are!"

At midnight, heavy rustling noises startle Fatima and her grandfather. A huge gray shape and two smaller ones can be seen by the light of the moon.

"Elephants," whispers Fatima.

"Elephants?" says Grandfather. "There haven't been elephants here in centuries."

Yet, there they are: a mother and her two babies. With every step, the hungry animals crush everything in their path.

Quickly! They must be stopped. Fatima hesitates. Grandfather does too. How can they frighten away such big and greedy beasts?

They make loud noises with pots and pans.
Bang! Bang! Bang!
They drench them with buckets of water.
Splash! Splash! Splash!
They throw pistachios at them.
Ping! Ping! Ping!

Nothing works. The elephants
continue to trample the orchard
until sunrise.

Wet and tired, Fatima sinks onto her bed. All her efforts to save the clementines have failed.

Even the spiders know that tomorrow, the elephants will return. And the day after that, and the day after that … until there is nothing left of the orchard.

"But how can we stop them?" cries Fatima. "They are so big and we are so small."

Fatima and Grandfather head to the market to ask for advice.

"You must kill the elephants with a gun!"

"You must trap them with a snare!"

"You must poison them with venom!"

"You must shoot them with arrows!"

Fear streaks across Fatima's heart as Grandfather decides to trade his last coins for a rifle and three bullets.

The trip back home is heavy with silence.

Fatima's heart beats fast.

She understands that they have to protect the orchard.

She also understands that the elephants shouldn't die.

Fatima pleads:

"The elephants aren't breaking our trees on purpose! Maybe we can find another way to stop them?"

"I'm afraid there's only one answer. We've already tried everything humanly possible …"

Fatima runs to find her friends the spiders.

"Grandfather is right! We have tried everything humanly possible. But you are not human!" She laughs. "I have a plan. It will only succeed if we work together. In return, I will peel clementines for you every day. Will you help me?"

The spiders agree. Immediately, Fatima plans a wonderful dance around the trees.

"Follow me and spin! Spin! Spin!!" she shouts.

As expected, at midnight, the elephants return. But what awaits them is breath-taking ...

A thick wall of spider webs is blocking their way.
Confused, the elephants circle the orchard and
slowly go back to the bush. They will never return.

Joy and relief brighten Grandfather's wrinkled face:

"You have saved the orchard!"

"AND we saved the elephants," adds Fatima, proudly.

"You may be small, but what you have done is very big."

Little by little, Fatima and her grandfather repair the broken trees and plant new ones. And since they no longer need it, even the rifle has a new use!

True to her word, Fatima thanks her friends the spiders by giving them peeled clementines every day.

"Hooray for little spiders!" shouts Fatima.

"Yes! And hooray for clever little girls too," says Grandfather.

When spider webs unite, they can stop elephants
—African proverb

Published in the United States in 2017 by Red Deer Press,
311 Washington Street, Brighton, Massachusetts 02135

Published in Canada by Red Deer Press,
195 Allstate Parkway, Markham, Ontario L3R 4T8

First published as Fatima et les voleurs de clémentines by Les Éditions de La Bagnole, 2012
© Mireille Messier, Gabrielle Grimard et les Éditions de la Bagnole, 2012

All inquiries should be addressed to Red Deer Press,
195 Allstate Parkway, Markham, Ontario L3R 4T8.
reddeerpress.com

10 9 8 7 6 5 4 3 2 1

Red Deer Press acknowledges with thanks the Canada Council for the Arts, and the Ontario Arts Council
for their support of our publishing program. We acknowledge the financial support of the Government of Canada
through the Canada Book Fund (CBF) for our publishing activities.

Library and Archives Canada Cataloguing in Publication

Messier, Mireille, 1971-
[Fatima et les voleurs de clémentines. English]
Fatima and the clementine thieves / Mireille Messier ; illustrator,
Gabrielle Grimard.

Translation of: Fatima et les voleurs de clémentines.
Translated by the author.
ISBN 978-0-88995-529-5 (bound)

I. Grimard, Gabrielle, 1975-, illustrator II. Title. III. Title: Fatima et les voleurs de clémentines. English.

PS8576.E7737F3713 2017   jC843'.54   C2015-904194-5

Publisher Cataloging-in-Publication Data (U.S)

Messier, Mireille, 1971-
Fatima and the clementine thieves / Mireille Messier ; illustrations by Gabrielle Grimard.
Originally published in French as: Fatima et les voleurs de clémentines.
[32] pages : color illustrations ; cm.
Summary: "One morning, Fatima and her grandfather wake up to find their clementine orchard savagely ransacked.
A little girl faces an ENORMOUS problem. Luckily, Fatima has powerful friends: the spiders" – Provided by publisher.
ISBN: 978-0-88995-529-5 (pbk.)
1. Grandparent and child – Juvenile fiction. 2. Spiders – Juvenile fiction. I. Grimard, Gabrielle. II. Title.
[E] dc23 PZ7.M4884Fa 2017

English translation: Mireille Messier
Edited for the Press by Peter Carver

Printed in China by Regent